THIS BOOK BELONGS TO

It was Christmas Eve.

The little girl got a present from her uncle.

She was very happy and unwrapped her present quickly.

It was a nutcracker doll.

The little girl loved her present straight away.

There was also a naughty little boy, and he was jealous, and destroyed the little girl's doll.

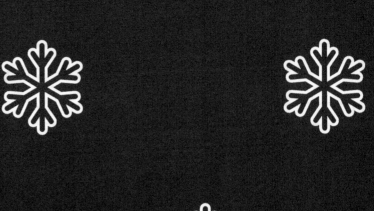

Luckily, her uncle quickly fixed the doll.

The girl was happy that it was possible to fix the nutcracker.

The girl kept her doll close all the time.

Something strange happened suddenly at night. The Rat King appeared in the living room.

Rats started running from all over.

The rats surrounded the little girl.

The nutcracker defended her and defeated the Rat King.

The little girl and the nutcracker started dancing.

The nutcracker suddenly turned into a prince. The little girl became a princess.

The prince and the princess went to candy land.

The little girl woke up in the living room the next morning. It was a dream. She remembered that magical Christmas Eve forever.

MERRY CHRISTMAS

Thank you for choosing us.
If this book made a good impression on you, please
leave us a comment on the purchase page.
It will help us grow and create new books for you.
All the best!

SCAN ME

Other Book in This Series
Gymnastics Coloring Book For Girls

Look Inside

Obraz autorstwa <a href="https://pl.freepik.com/darmowe-wektory/recznie-rysowane-plaska-kolekcja-dziadek-do-orzechow-swiatecznych_19851209.htm#query=nutcracker&position=41&from_view=search&track=sph">Freepik</a

<a href="https://www.vecteezy.com/vector-art/9101150-illustration-of-princess-design-elements">Illustration of princess design elements Vectors by Vecteezy</a>

<a href="https://www.vecteezy.com/vector-art/3589161-christmas-holiday-party-background-happy-new-year-and-merry-christmas-poster">Christmas Holiday Party Background. Happy New Year and Merry Christmas Poster Vectors by Vecteezy</a>

<a href="https://www.vecteezy.com/vector-art/8823033-christmas-boy-opening-gift-coloring-page-for-kids">Christmas Boy Opening Gift Coloring Page for Kids Vectors by Vecteezy</a>

<a href="https://www.vecteezy.com/vector-art/4328839-cute-girl-holding-present-christmas-coloring-page-for-kid">cute girl holding present christmas coloring page for kid Vectors by Vecteezy</a>

<a href="https://www.vecteezy.com/vector-art/10913126-man-waving-with-laptop">Man waving with laptop Vectors by Vecteezy</a>

<a href="https://www.vecteezy.com/vector-art/519842-a-girl-sleeping-in-bed">A girl sleeping in bed Vectors by Vecteezy</a>

Obraz autorstwa <a href="https://pl.freepik.com/darmowe-wektory/recznie-rysowane-swiateczne-dekoracje-pakiet_5882808.htm#page=2&query=garland&position=0&from_view=search&track=sph">Freepik</a>

<a href="https://www.vecteezy.com/vector-art/7741775-vector-illustrations-of-mouse-characters-in-various-medieval-outfits">Vector illustrations of Mouse characters in various medieval outfits. Vectors by Vecteezy</a>

<a href="https://www.vecteezy.com/vector-art/1920680-princess-with-prince-fairytale-avatar-character">princess with prince fairytale avatar character Vectors by Vecteezy</a>

<a href="https://www.vecteezy.com/vector-art/10789352-christmas-tree-coloring-page-colored-illustration">Christmas Tree Coloring Page Colored Illustration Vectors by Vecteezy</a>

<a href="https://www.vecteezy.com/vector-art/5084549-big-family-with-three-generation">Big family with three generation Vectors by Vecteezy</a>

<a href="https://www.vecteezy.com/vector-art/2752361-ballet-ballerina-s-legs-in-a-tutu-and-pointe-line-art">Ballet. Ballerina's legs in a tutu and pointe. Line art. Vectors by Vecteezy</a>

<a href="https://pl.freepik.com/darmowe-wektory/zestaw-naklejek-naiwnych-tancerzy-baletowych_32477424.htm#query=ballet&position=49&from_view=search&track=sph">Obraz autorstwa pikisuperstar</a> na Freepik

<a href="https://www.vecteezy.com/vector-art/8823021-christmas-ornament-coloring-page-for-kids">Christmas Ornament Coloring Page for Kids Vectors by Vecteezy</a>

<a href="https://www.vecteezy.com/vector-art/8944125-christmas-gifts-coloring-page-for-kids">Christmas Gifts Coloring Page for Kids Vectors by Vecteezy</a>

<a href="https://www.vecteezy.com/vector-art/8944220-christmas-snow-globe-isolated-coloring-page">Christmas Snow Globe Isolated Coloring Page Vectors by Vecteezy</a>

<a href="https://www.vecteezy.com/vector-art/2454738-cute-granfather-member-seated-in-sofa-character">cute granfather member seated in sofa character Vectors by Vecteezy</a>

<a href="https://www.vecteezy.com/vector-art/1053526-father-and-his-son-sleeping-together">Father and his son sleeping together Vectors by Vecteezy</a>

<a href="https://pl.freepik.com/darmowe-wektory/izometryczny-schemat-blokowy-baletu-z-ilustracji-wektorowych-wykonawcow-teatru-i-tanca_32745019.htm#query=ballet&position=46&from_view=search&track=sph">Obraz autorstwa macrovector</a> na Freepik

<a href="https://www.vecteezy.com/vector-art/8944179-christmas-wreath-with-bells-isolated-coloring">Christmas Wreath With Bells Isolated Coloring Vectors by Vecteezy</a>

<a href="https://www.vecteezy.com/vector-art/8944275-christmas-stocking-house-isolated-coloring-page">Christmas Stocking House Isolated Coloring Page Vectors by Vecteezy</a>

<a href="https://www.vecteezy.com/vector-art/8944079-christmas-gingerbread-house-coloring-page">Christmas Gingerbread House Coloring Page Vectors by Vecteezy</a>

<a href="https://www.vecteezy.com/vector-art/299678-little-girl-sitting-in-arm-chair">Little girl sitting in arm chair Vectors by Vecteezy</a>

<a href="https://www.vecteezy.com/vector-art/540051-happy-kids-illustration">Happy Kids Illustration Vectors by Vecteezy</a>

Made in the USA
Monee, IL
25 October 2024

68680494R00037